The Little Lost Cloud

PAUL GORRY

For Keiko, Luca and Franco.

Even though you're a little too old to read this now.

A little cloud was way up high.
He floated high up in the sky...

He saw the sea, he saw the boats,
He wondered how the boats could float?

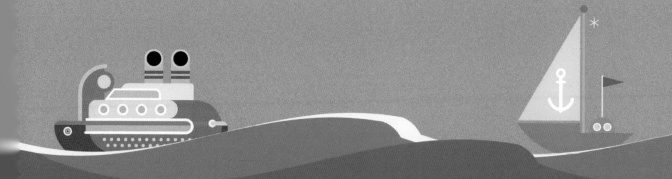

The bigger clouds just didn't care.
But little cloud, he had to stare!

He saw a pier, he saw the beach.
Way down below, beyond his reach...

Ooohhh! What's this?

And this...

He saw a town, and people too!
With lots of traffic moving through...

And then the ground moved up to him.
The bigger clouds began to grin!

A little drop, a bigger drop.
The bigger clouds, they rained a lot!

But little cloud, he squeezed and squeezed.
He couldn't rain...he huffed and wheezed.

What's happening to the bigger clouds?

Oh no, they're shrinking!

And one by one, they dissapeared...

The little cloud thought that this was weird....

Then little cloud was all alone.
The bigger clouds were all he'd known.

And then he saw the sea again.
With sand and waves and boats, and then...

Little clouds, all around.
Left and right, and up and down...

And he was big, and they were small?
How could this be? He starts to call...

But then he saw the land again.
The ground moved up to him AND THEN!

A little drop, a bigger drop...
The little cloud he rained a lot!

The sea had made him big you see...

And hills had set the water free.

THE END

Printed in Great Britain
by Amazon